the Milo & Jazz MYSTERIES®

5

THE CASE OF THE JULY 4TH JINX

by Lewis B. Montgomery
illustrated by Amy Wummer

The KANE PRESS
New York

Text copyright © 2010 by Lewis B. Montgomery
Illustrations copyright © 2010 by Amy Wummer
Super Sleuthing Strategies original illustrations copyright © 2010 by Kane Press, Inc.
Super Sleuthing Strategies original illustrations by Nadia DiMattia

Library of Congress Cataloging-in-Publication Data

Montgomery, Lewis B.
The case of the July 4th jinx / by Lewis B. Montgomery ;
illustrated by Amy Wummer.
p. cm. — (The Milo & Jazz mysteries ; 5)
Summary: With the help of ace detective Dash Marlowe, sleuths-in-training
Milo and Jazz investigate a so-called jinx at the local Fourth of July fair.
ISBN 978-1-57565-315-0 (library binding : alk. paper) — ISBN 978-1-57565-308-2
(pbk. : alk. paper) [1. Luck—Fiction. 2. Fairs—Fiction. 3. Fourth of July—Fiction.
4. Mystery and detective stories.] I. Wummer, Amy, ill. II. Title. III.
Title: Case of the July fourth jinx.
PZ7.M7682Caj 2010
[Fic]—dc22
2009049886
ISBN 978-1-57565-362-4 (e-book)

3 5 7 9 10 8 6 4 2

First published in the United States of America in 2010 by Kane Press, Inc.
Printed at Worzalla Publishing, Stevens Point, WI, U.S.A., May 2012.

Book Design: Edward Miller

The Milo & Jazz Mysteries is a registered trademark of Kane Press, Inc.

Visit us online at www.kanepress.com

 Like us on Facebook
facebook.com/kanepress

 Follow us on Twitter
@kanepress

For the wonderful staff of the
Louisa Gonser Community Library
—L.B.M.

CHAPTER ONE

Milo stared at the white-frosted cake topped with tiny American flags. More frosting, red and blue, spelled out *Happy Fourth of July*. So much frosting . . .

The Fourth wasn't until tomorrow. That must be why the cake hadn't been cut into slices like everything else on the bake-sale table. It still looked perfect.

Perfectly delicious.

His finger inched toward it. Nobody would miss a tiny dab. . . .

"Looks real, doesn't it?" The teenage boy by the table grinned down at Milo. His official fair badge said WINSTON.

"It isn't real?" Milo asked.

"Nope, just for show," the boy said. "All the rest is real, though. I promise."

Milo glanced at his friend Jazz. She was looking at the pies with his brother, Ethan. Lucky she hadn't caught him being

fooled by a fake cake. After all, detectives were supposed to be careful observers!

Jazz and Milo were detectives in training. They got lessons by mail from world-famous private eye Dash Marlowe. With a little help from Dash, they had already cracked a few real-life cases.

"Milo," Ethan called across the table. "Can I have this?"

He pointed to a
slice of chocolate pie.

Winston beamed.
"Made that one
myself! Chocolate-cookie
cream pie. My new recipe."

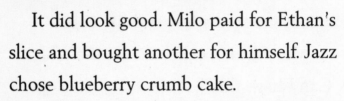

It did look good. Milo paid for Ethan's
slice and bought another for himself. Jazz
chose blueberry crumb cake.

As Milo took his slice, a ride called
the Scream Machine started up noisily
behind him. Startled, he spun around.
The pie slid off its paper plate and
splattered on the ground.

"Oh, no!" he moaned.

Winston shook his head in sympathy.
"Looks like the jinx has struck again."

"The jinx?" Milo asked.

"People are saying that the fair is jinxed this year," Winston explained. "Because of all the weird stuff that's been happening."

"Weird stuff?" Jazz said. "Like what?"

"Oh . . . like all the entries for the Hottest Chili Pepper contest disappeared. Then they turned up later in a box marked Fireworks."

"I'm going to stay up and watch the fireworks this year," Ethan told Winston. "And I'm not going to be scared."

Milo rolled his eyes. His little brother had said the same thing last year. But as always, at the first big *BOOM*, Ethan had burst into tears and the whole family had had to go home.

"What else has gone wrong?" Jazz asked Winston.

"Well, some kiddie-farm animals got loose." Winston made a face. "Do you have any clue how hard it is to catch a pig?"

Milo glanced at Jazz. He was thinking of her pet pig, Bitsy. "Actually—"

"And Uncle Sam keeps losing air, but nobody can find a leak." Winston pointed

toward a giant inflated Uncle Sam bobbing gently in the breeze.

Milo took a look around. Sun sparkled off the game-booth roofs. He could smell the kettle corn and hear the shrieks of terror from the Scream Machine. Everything seemed perfectly normal. Could the fair really be jinxed?

"I just hope nothing goes wrong at the prize judging tomorrow," Winston said. "Or the parade." He handed Milo a new slice of pie and waved away his money. "It's on me."

Milo took a bite. *Mmmm.* Creamy . . . crunchy . . . chocolatey . . .

Suddenly something slammed into his elbow. The pie flew from his hand—

SPLAT.

CHAPTER TWO

"Hey!" Milo protested. "That was my . . ."

Whoa.

His voice trailed off as he stared up at the boy who had bumped his elbow. Wow. The kid was *huge.*

He didn't seem to have noticed Milo at all. Laughing and shoving with his buddies, the boy lumbered off into the crowd.

"HOOLIGANS!" a voice shrieked.

A woman was storming toward the bake-sale table, clutching a foil-covered pie tin. She glared after the group of boys. "SCOUNDRELS! RAPSCALLIONS!"

A man with a mustache jogged up behind her. Milo recognized him: the chief of police. Chief Smalley visited their school every year to talk about putting trash in its place and stuff like that.

"Now, Mom," the chief said to the woman. "I'm sure they didn't mean—"

She swung around on him. "Those young roughnecks nearly knocked this pie right out of my hands, Jeffrey! My PRIZE-WINNING LEMON PIE!"

His mustache twitching nervously, Chief Smalley took the pie and set it on

the table. He peeled off the foil cover. "It's just fine. See? No harm done."

Milo wished his chocolate pie had been that lucky.

"I'll bet it will sell quicker than anything on the table," the chief went on.

His mother still looked furious. "What if that had been tomorrow's pie? The one I enter in THE CONTEST?"

She marched off, her son trailing after. "But Mom . . ."

Winston began slicing the pie to sell it, and Jazz picked up the labeled foil.

"Mrs. Smalley's Luscious Lemon Pie," she read aloud. "Blue Ribbon Winner, Three Years Running."

Milo whistled. "Must be good."

Winston stopped cutting. "Maybe it is, maybe it isn't."

"What do you mean?" Milo asked. "Didn't she really win three times?"

The older boy grinned. "Yeah, but guess who always judges the pie contest? The chief of police."

"You mean her own son is the judge?" Jazz said. "But that's not fair!"

Winston laughed and shrugged.

"Probably not. But who's going to tell *her* that?"

The Scream Machine ground to a stop, and riders streamed off. Milo spotted Spencer and Carlos, their friends from school, and he waved them over.

Spencer's face was greenish yellow.

"We went on the Scream Machine twice in a row," Carlos said. "It was great! Wasn't it great?" He pounded Spencer on the back.

Spencer wobbled.

A burst of applause came from a nearby stage. An announcer's voice boomed, "Next up, The Great Tripolini—"

"It's the juggling man!" Ethan pulled on Milo's arm. "Come on!"

Over by the stage, Milo saw the boy who had bumped into him. He was horsing around with some of his pals.

Carlos followed Milo's gaze and groaned. "Oh, no. It's the Zoo Crew."

"Zoo Crew?" Jazz repeated.

"That's what they call them at the middle school, 'cause they're so wild," Carlos explained. "The big one in the hat—that's Crash, their leader. My sister said he set the school on fire."

"For real?" Milo asked.

"Fire trucks and everything."

Spencer, closer to his usual color now, asked, "Are those the guys who flooded the boys' bathroom, and they had to close the school?"

Carlos nodded. "And did you hear about the farm stand?"

"Out at Goose Egg Farm?" Jazz asked.

"They knocked it over."

Milo gasped. *Whodunnit* magazine was always full of stories about bad guys "knocking over" banks.

"You mean they robbed it?" he asked.

Carlos gave him a funny look. "No, they knocked it over, like I said. Broken eggs and smashed tomatoes everywhere. It was ugly."

On the stage, the juggler finished up to a round of applause. A tall man bounded forward, microphone in hand.

"Thank you, The Great Tripolini! Now, let's have a big welcome for our next act: Viola Pritchett's School of Dance!"

A large, pink woman swept onstage. Behind her straggled a dozen little girls in purple flower costumes.

Viola Pritchett clasped her hands. "Today my flowers will dance to a dainty little tune I call—" She let out a tinkling laugh. "—*Viola's Violets.*"

Jazz made a gagging noise.

Viola fluttered her fingers toward the tall announcer, who popped a CD into the player and pressed a button.

For a moment there was only silence. Then a voice from the speakers howled, *"YOU'RE IN THE JUNGLE, BABY! AAAAAAAAAAAAAAHHHHHH!"*

CHAPTER THREE

Electric guitar and pounding drums
blasted out of the speakers and filled
the air. Leaping back, the announcer
crashed into Viola Pritchett as she rushed
forward. They fell into a tangled heap.

The little flower girls went wild,
shaking and stomping to the driving beat.
One slid across the stage on her knees as
the crowd hooted and cheered.

"Put your petals to the metal!" someone bellowed.

The announcer was struggling to get out from under Viola Pritchett. She pushed him back, then fell on top of him.

Spencer poked Milo and said, "That was a pancake slam! I saw it on *America's Craziest Wrestling.*"

Near the stage, the Zoo Crew was falling all over each other with laughter.

At last Viola Pritchett peeled herself off the announcer and yanked the cord to the CD player. The music stopped.

In the sudden silence, the girls froze. Then, after a look at their teacher's face, they scattered off the stage to thunderous applause.

A boy with a tuba took their place.

Jazz nudged Milo. "Let's get out of here. Last year that kid played 'Yankee Doodle Dandy' twenty minutes straight."

Pulling Ethan along, they squeezed their way through the crowd. Behind the stage, Milo saw the announcer arguing with Viola Pritchett.

"All I know is, the CD case said *Viola's Violets*!" the man was saying. "How was I supposed to tell it was the wrong CD inside?" He shook his head. "I've had enough of this fair. This switcheroo is the last straw."

Viola Pritchett put a large pink hand up to her forehead. "This is sabotage!" she cried.

"If you ask me," the man muttered, "it's the jinx."

As they walked away from the stage, Milo asked Jazz, "Do you think the fair is really jinxed?"

"I don't believe in jinxes," Jazz said firmly.

"Then how come so many things are going wrong? Animals getting loose, Uncle Sam losing air, hot peppers in the fireworks box . . . and now this."

"Any of those things could have been an accident," Jazz pointed out.

"Yeah," Milo said, "but that's a lot of accidents."

Jazz frowned. "I wonder if somebody could be doing it on purpose."

"You mean, like those pranks that Gordy pulls?" Milo asked.

Gordy Fletcher lived on Jazz's street and had been in their class last year. He loved playing jokes on people.

"Well, I can tell you it's not Gordy," Jazz said. "He's away visiting his grandma. We haven't found fake dog poop on our porch for weeks." She looked thoughtful. "Anyway, this seems like a bigger deal than Gordy's pranks."

"Viola Pritchett called it sabotage," Milo said.

"But who would want to mess with the Fourth of July fair?"

Their eyes met. Milo grinned.

"I think we've got a new case, partner," he said.

Jazz smiled too.

Then, suddenly, her smile disappeared.

"Milo . . . where's Ethan?"

Milo glanced to one side and then the other. He whipped around.

His little brother was nowhere in sight.

CHAPTER FOUR

"Ethan!" Milo called. "ETHAN!"

"Ethan!" Jazz echoed.

"I'll look around here," Milo said.

Jazz nodded. "And I'll check the kiddie rides. Let's meet back by Uncle Sam."

They split up, and Milo began searching the crowd.

"Lose something?" a voice asked.

It was Winston, the teenager from the bake-sale table.

"My brother ran off," Milo said.

"Little kid in a T-rex shirt?" Winston asked. "Don't worry. I just saw him."

Milo's heart jumped. "Where?"

"This way," Winston said, and Milo followed him around to the other side of a big tent. Winston pointed to the batting cage and smiled. "There he is."

Ethan stood just outside the cage, his ear pressed up against the wire fence. As Milo ran toward him, the ball flew toward the batter.

CRACK!

Ethan leaped away.

"What in the world are you doing?" Milo gasped as he came puffing up.

"I'm getting used to the loud noise,"
Ethan explained, "so I can watch the
fireworks tomorrow night and not be
scared." He pressed his ear up to the
fence again.

CRACK!

Milo yanked his brother away from the batting cage.

"I've been looking all over for you," he scolded. He turned to thank Winston, but the older boy had left.

Keeping a firm grip on Ethan's arm, Milo steered him down the hill. On the way, he saw Crash and the Zoo Crew by the kiddie farm. They were mooing at the cow.

Jazz was waiting by the giant Uncle Sam. "You found him! Where was he?"

"At the batting cage," Milo told her. "And you won't believe—"

Jazz's eyes widened. She pointed to something over Milo's shoulder. "Look!"

He turned, and blinked.

A flock of chickens rocketed down the hill. Behind the chickens came a swarm of people yelling, "Catch them!"

Chief Smalley and the man from the kiddie farm were in the lead. As Milo watched, they each lunged toward a chicken and went sprawling.

"FEATHERED FIENDS!" a voice

shrieked. Mrs. Smalley came charging
down the hill. Squawking in terror, the
flock scattered, feathers flying. One
chicken rose up and headed straight
toward Jazz, Ethan, and Milo.

"Duck!" Jazz shouted.

As Milo pulled him down, Ethan said,
"That's a chicken, not a duck!"

The chicken flapped over their heads and skidded into Uncle Sam. Frantically, it dug in its claws. There was a loud pop, then a long, low hiss.

Uncle Sam swayed and shrank, finally collapsing in a giant, floppy heap.

Stunned, the chicken gave up. The man from the kiddie farm grabbed it, then quickly rounded up the rest of the flock.

Milo looked at Jazz. "Guess we know how Uncle Sam lost his air this time."

Jazz laughed. "Guess so." She added, "But how did the chickens get loose?"

Hmm. Good question.

"Let's check out the chicken coop," Milo said. "Maybe we can find a clue."

They headed uphill, toward the bake-sale table, where Winston and Chief Smalley had joined forces against a stray chicken and a goat. The goat seemed to think the tablecloth looked as delicious as the cake. Milo and Jazz stopped to help, but the chief waved them off.

At the kiddie farm, the flock was settling down. Jazz examined the latch on the chicken coop. "Looks fine to me," she said. "And I don't see any way

it could be opened
from inside. So,
either the chickens
are magicians . . ."

"Or somebody let
them out," Milo finished.

Jazz nodded. "And I'll bet it's the same
somebody who's behind the rest of this
so-called jinx."

Just then, they heard yelling in the
distance.

"Not again!" Milo said. "What now?"

Jazz turned. "I think it's coming from
the ball pit."

Milo tried to make sense out of the
hubbub. Then a single word cut through.

"SNAKE!"

CHAPTER Five

Milo and Jazz rushed toward the noise, with Ethan close behind. They saw little kids pouring out of a pit filled with brightly colored plastic balls.

Jazz caught hold of a small boy. "What happened?"

"There's a snake in there! I saw it!" Pulling free, the boy ran to his mother.

Milo scanned the crowd. The ball pit was empty now. The kids were jumping around in their socks, chattering excitedly. All but one.

To the side, a girl about Ethan's age sat calmly strapping on her sandals. She had chocolate smears on her face, and she was . . . smiling?

Milo and Jazz exchanged a glance.

Striding up to the girl, Milo demanded, "How come you're the only one who isn't scared?"

The girl looked up. Her smile faded.

"You did it, didn't you?" he accused.

"It was just a joke," she said.

"A joke?" Jazz said from behind Milo. "Letting a snake loose?"

The girl's lower lip trembled. "Only a *rubber* snake. He said it would be funny."

Milo and Jazz looked at each other.

"Who?" Milo asked.

"The *boy*," she said. "The big boy." Then her eyes widened. "Uh-oh."

A woman wearing a fair badge climbed out of the ball pit with a long, lifelike rubber snake. She did not look happy.

Nearby, Milo spotted the Zoo Crew watching and laughing. Crash towered in the center of the group. *The big boy.*

Eagerly, Milo turned back to the girl. "Was that the—"

But she was gone.

"Where did that girl go?" he asked Jazz, who was watching the woman with the snake.

"Huh?" Jazz turned. "Oh, no! She was here a second ago!"

"Look who *is* here, though." Milo pointed to the Zoo Crew.

Jazz's eyes narrowed. "Weren't they at the stage watching Viola's Violets, too?"

He nodded. "That's what I was thinking. Carlos said they're always making trouble. . . ."

"And this fair has had a lot of trouble."

Before Jazz could say anything more, Crash elbowed one of the boys next to him and jerked his head toward the exit. The Zoo Crew moved off.

"Let's follow them!" Jazz said.

"But I want to go in the ball pit," Ethan protested.

"Later," Milo said, hauling him along.

With Ethan hanging back and digging in his heels, they quickly lost ground. Soon the Zoo Crew vanished in the crowd, as Milo fumed.

Then, coming straight toward them, Milo saw the most beautiful sight ever: his mom and dad.

He shoved his little brother at them, babbling a quick excuse. Then he and Jazz set off.

"There they are!" Jazz pointed toward the exit gate.

"Let's go!" Milo said.

He and Jazz trailed the Zoo Crew out of the fairgrounds. They tried to stay close enough not to lose them again, but far enough back not to be noticed.

Suddenly the Zoo Crew ducked down an alley. Milo and Jazz broke into a run. But by the time they reached the turn, the boys had disappeared.

CHAPTER SIX

"Look!" Jazz nudged Milo.

Halfway down the alley, a garage door was just rolling shut.

They crept toward the garage.

Milo peeked in. "I can't see anything. It's just black."

"I think they taped garbage bags over the windows," Jazz whispered.

Around the back they found another window, also covered. But it was open a crack. They could hear noises coming from inside.

Jazz put a finger to her lips.

First Milo heard a scraping sound, then a few thumps. Somebody said, "Looks like we're good to go."

"I can't believe we're doing this," said another voice. "If anyone finds out it's us . . ."

"Life as we know it will be over," someone else finished.

"You guys worry too much," the first voice said. "Nobody will know it's us. Anyway, it's too late to back out now. Tomorrow is the Fourth."

"We still haven't got a shrimpy kid," one of the boys grumbled.

"How about your brother?"

"No way, Crash. The kid's a snitch. Besides, he's small for a sixth grader, but not that small. I don't think he'd fit."

Crash sighed. "Maybe we'll just have to do it without the kid."

A door slammed nearby. Milo jumped.

Jazz whispered, "We'd better go."

They tiptoed away from the garage. Once they reached the alley they ran, not slowing down until a stitch in Milo's side forced him to stop. Collapsing on the sidewalk, he gasped, "Holy cow."

"They're definitely up to something," Jazz agreed. "Did you hear what they said about the Fourth of July?"

Milo nodded. "They *must* be the ones behind the jinx. And tomorrow they're going to pull something big—"

"But what?" Jazz asked. "And why do they need a small kid?"

Small enough to fit.

Milo jumped to his feet. "Listen. Once I read a story in *Whodunnit* magazine about a gang of robbers and a little kid—"

"I read that one too!" Jazz broke in. "The robbers pushed the kid in through a window because they were all too big to fit . . ." She paused. "You think the Zoo Crew is planning a break-in at the fair?"

Milo shrugged. "Tomorrow everyone will be at the prize-judging tent and then watching the parade. The rest of the fair will be practically empty."

"If only we had some kind of proof that they're behind the pranks," Jazz said. "I wish we knew what they're hiding in that garage."

"We could sneak in after dark."

Jazz shook her head. "If we got caught, we'd be in real trouble."

Feeling stuck, the two detectives split up and headed home for dinner.

Milo carried in the mail and dropped it on the table. An envelope with *DM* in the corner slipped out of the stack.

A detective lesson from Dash Marlowe!

DASH MARLOWE

SECRETS OF A SUPER SLEUTH!

Role Play

A mild-mannered bank clerk stays past closing time—and blows the safe.

A Boy Scout helps you cross a busy street—and picks your pocket on the way.

At the post office, you see your friendly next-door neighbor—on a WANTED poster!

Many people are not what they seem. As a detective, sometimes you have to fight fire with fire—by pretending to be someone you're not. In other words: go undercover.

Going undercover means convincing your suspects you are one of them. To do this, you need to play a role. The way you act, the way you speak, the way you look—it's all part of your disguise.

If you play your role well and get your suspects to trust you, they may let clues slip. And if you play it *really* well, you may even learn to think like your suspects—and that can help you solve the crime.

Just don't forget who you really are, or you may find yourself in hot water. That happened to me once, when I was investigating dirty deeds at a Laundromat. But that's another story. . . .

Milo folded up the lesson, stuck it in his pocket, and smiled.

He knew exactly what to do.

CHAPTER SEVEN

Just after breakfast, the doorbell rang. It was Jazz.

"Yo," Milo said. "What's poppin', dawg?"

She stared at him. "Where did you get that giant shirt?"

"My dad. I tried to wear his pants, too, but they fell all the way down."

"Wow," she said. "You look really . . ."

"Cool?" Milo asked.

Jazz reached over and turned his baseball cap around so it pointed forward. "No—ridiculous. What's it for?"

"I'm going undercover with the Zoo Crew," he said. "We need to find out what they've got planned—and stop them before it's too late."

He handed her the lesson from Dash.

She read it, then shook her head. "I don't know, Milo. It seems risky. What if they figure out what you're up to?"

"How could they? My disguise is perfect. Those Zoo Crew guys will think I'm off the chain."

"They'll think you're off your rocker," Jazz said. "Besides, I didn't hear them talking the way you're talking."

"The Zoo Crew kids are tough," Milo explained. "This is how tough guys talk. I saw it on TV!"

Jazz gave him a look. "This is just so . . . not you."

"It's the new me," he told her. "Rough. Tough. Fearless—"

BAM!

He screamed and jumped.

Jazz stared up at the ceiling. "What was *that*?"

"ETHAN!" he yelled.

His brother leaned over the stair rail. "Yeah?"

"What was that noise?"

"I dropped a book."

Milo just looked at him.

"Well, it was the big fat dictionary,"

Ethan said. "And
I was standing on
a chair."

"And holding it
up over your head?"
Jazz asked.

Ethan grinned.
"I wasn't scared at all! I think I'm almost
ready for the fireworks tonight."

He vanished. A moment later, another
crash shook the ceiling.

"He's driving me nuts," Milo said.
"Slamming doors. Dropping heavy stuff.
Popping balloons . . ."

Jazz wasn't listening.

"Milo," she said, "I was thinking. That
girl at the ball pit is an eyewitness. She's
the only one we know who's actually

seen the boy who's pulling all those pranks. She can tell us if Crash got her to put that rubber snake in the ball pit. We need to find her again."

"Good idea," he said. "You look for her, and I'll go undercover. Let's meet at the fair at noon."

She gave his disguise one last doubtful look. "Are you sure you want to do this?"

"For shizzle, dawg."

Jazz winced. "Milo, please quit saying 'dawg.' And pull your pants up."

"But showing underwear makes you look tough," Milo protested. "Everyone knows that."

"Not when the underwear has happy penguins on it."

He looked down. Oops.

Hitching up his jeans, he saw her out and then took off for the Zoo Crew's hideout. When he got there, it was still and silent. Had they already left for the fair?

He circled around to the back. The window near the ground was closed tight. But then he spotted an open window high up on the garage wall.

A metal trash can sat nearby. He tugged it over and climbed up on the lid—

"What do you think you're doing?"

The lid flew out from under Milo. With a bang and a clatter, he tumbled off. The trash can fell on top of him.

Sprawled in the dirt, he looked up at the unsmiling faces of the Zoo Crew.

Uh-oh.

Weakly, Milo stuck out his hand for a
fist bump. "Um . . . yo?"

They stared down at him in silence.

He tried to look tough. "Word on the
street is that you're looking for a kid
who's small enough to fit."

Crash folded his huge arms and glanced around. "Okay, who blabbed?"

"Not me, Crash!" one of the boys said.

"Me neither."

"*I* kept my mouth shut."

Milo pushed himself to his feet. "Anyway, what's the difference? You can use me, right?"

Crash eyed him for a long moment. "How do we know you won't blab?"

"Why would I blab? I'll be in on it too." Realizing what he'd just said, Milo gulped. If it all went wrong, would he end up in jail?

Crash looked around at the others. "He *is* about the right size. And we're out of time."

"We don't need him," a boy said.

"Yeah, we do," Crash told him. "No way am I going to be the only fruit."

The only . . . *what?*

"I'm a tomato," another boy said. "That's a fruit."

"No, that's a vegetable."

"Oh, yeah? My mother said—"

Vegetables? Fruits? Milo broke in. "What are you talking about?"

"What do you think?" Crash said. "Our costumes."

"Costumes? For what?"

"For this."

Crash gave the garage door a powerful heave. The door rolled up.

Sunlight flooded into the dark space. And at last, Milo saw what the Zoo Crew had been hiding.

CHAPTER EIGHT

It was a basket. A basket with handles, the kind people might use for a picnic or to carry home their vegetables. But this basket was the size of a truck. And it had wheels.

"Wh-what *is* that?" Milo stammered.

"Our float," Crash said. "For the parade."

A float? The Zoo Crew's big secret was a *float*?

Misreading the stunned look on Milo's face, Crash said, "It looks a lot better with us in it, in our costumes."

"Oh . . ." Milo said faintly.

Crash dug in a box and began flinging costumes to the waiting boys—tomato, carrot, eggplant, ear of corn. He tossed one to Milo, too. "You're the strawberry."

Milo held it up. "It's . . . it's *pink*."

"It was supposed to be a beet," the tomato explained, fluffing up his stuffing. "But it shrank in the wash. So Crash said we could add a stem and paint on seeds and have it be a strawberry."

The eggplant put in, "We just needed to find a kid small enough—"

"To fit in the costume," Milo finished. Oh, boy. And here he had been thinking

that the Zoo Crew was planning a break-in!

"But why the big secret?" he asked.

Zipping himself up, the carrot snorted. "Are you kidding? If anyone finds out we dressed up like a bunch of vegetables, we'll never live it down."

Milo's head was spinning. "Then why are you doing it?"

Slowly, the other vegetables turned and stared hard at Crash.

"Come on," Crash protested. "I didn't knock over the farm stand all by myself. You guys ran right into it, too."

"Yeah," the eggplant said. "But we wouldn't have been running if that mama goose hadn't been chasing us."

The ear of corn added, "And she was

only chasing us because you ran off with her baby."

"I guess I should have put it down," Crash admitted, climbing into a gigantic watermelon costume. "But it's hard to think straight when a big, mean, hissing goose is after you."

"That mama goose was pretty mad," the corn agreed.

Gloomily, the carrot said, "Not half as mad as the farm lady when her eggs and vegetables went flying."

"We offered to pay her back by working on the farm," Crash told Milo. "But for some reason she didn't want us there. That's why we have to wear the veggie costumes. She said if we did a Goose Egg Farm float for the parade, she wouldn't call our parents."

"So . . . you didn't knock over the farm stand on purpose?" Milo asked.

"Of course not," the watermelon said. "Why would we do a thing like that?"

"Well . . . I mean . . ." Milo hesitated. "What about all that other stuff you did? Like setting fire to the school?"

"There wasn't any fire," the corn said.

"Just lots of smoke. Crash had this bright idea about using the Bunsen burners in the science lab to make s'mores."

Milo asked, "And the boys' room flood . . . ?"

"No time to talk about that now," Crash cut in hastily. "The farmer will be here soon. And you're still not dressed."

Milo looked at the strawberry costume in his hand. It was so . . . pink. He sighed. When he'd decided to go undercover, this was not exactly what he'd had in mind.

As Milo zipped himself into the costume, the farmer arrived in her tractor to hook up the float. She joked with the Zoo Crew cheerfully. Now that they were paying her back, she seemed to have forgiven them for the farm-stand disaster.

The boys piled on the float, and the tractor moved off slowly down the alley.

As they rode toward the fairgrounds, Milo puzzled over what he had learned. The Zoo Crew was not at all what he'd expected. Could they be behind the trouble at the fair? It didn't seem likely. But if they weren't the culprits, who was?

The tractor rolled into the fairgrounds. The prize judging seemed to have started. Near the tent, at the edge of the crowd, Milo spotted Jazz. Then he saw who was standing beside her.

It was the rubber-snake girl.

CHAPTER NINE

Milo hurtled off the float and charged toward the two girls, shouting, "Jazz!"

They glanced up. Jazz looked startled. The smaller girl screamed and hid behind her. "It's a monster strawberry!"

"Milo? Is that you?" Jazz asked. "What are you doing in that costume?"

"Helping out the Zoo Crew," he said. "It's a long story."

Jazz shot a glance over his shoulder.

"*That's* the Zoo Crew?" she asked.

Milo turned and saw a herd of produce stampeding toward them. The girl peeped out from behind Jazz, squeaked in terror, and hid again.

As the Zoo Crew screeched to a halt, Jazz hauled the girl back out. She pointed to the watermelon, towering over all the others. "The big one! Crash! Did he give you the snake?"

The girl stared wide-eyed at the giant fruit.

The watermelon turned to Milo. "What's she talking about?"

Milo said, "Jazz, I don't think—"

"THIEVES!" a familiar voice shrieked. "BANDITS! HIGHWAY ROBBERY!"

Mrs. Smalley stood at the front of the tent stabbing her finger at an empty spot on the table.

"MY PIE IS GONE!"

Jazz whirled on the Zoo Crew. "You! What did you do with that pie?"

"Huh? Us? We didn't do anything!"

"They couldn't have," Milo said. "They've been with me all morning."

Suddenly the girl piped up. *"That's him!"*

Everyone turned. The girl pointed. "There! Way up front! Next to the yelling lady! He gave me the snake!"

Milo looked. *"Chief Smalley?"*

"No, silly. The boy. The big boy."

It was Winston.

Jazz stared at the girl. "*He* gave you the rubber snake to put into the ball pit?"

The girl nodded happily. "And a piece of chocolate pie."

"Oh, man," Crash said from inside his watermelon costume. "That guy makes the best pie ever. I could not believe he didn't win first prize last year."

"Second place three years in a row," the eggplant added mournfully.

Jazz stared at them. Then at Winston. Then at Mrs. Smalley, who by now had turned as purple as the eggplant.

"So, Winston was the prankster. . . ." she said slowly. "And his pie lost out to Mrs. Smalley's, three years in a row. . . ."

"And now Mrs. Smalley's pie is missing!" Milo said.

They stared at each other. He knew they were thinking the same thing.

Milo and Jazz pushed their way forward. The Zoo Crew scrambled after them. At the sight of fruits and vegetables on the march, the crowd fell silent.

Jazz faced Winston and announced, "You took Mrs. Smalley's pie."

All eyes turned to Winston.

"Wh-wh-why would I do that?" he stammered.

"I think you were sick of Mrs. Smalley always winning first prize, just because the pie judge is her son," Jazz said.

Now all eyes turned to Chief Smalley.

His mustache twitched. He cleared his throat, but didn't say anything.

"JEFFREY!" Mrs. Smalley howled. "Are you just going to stand there and let her insult my Luscious Lemon Pie?"

Ignoring her, Jazz said to Winston, "With Mrs. Smalley's pie out of the contest, the other pies would have a chance to win. But—"

Milo jumped in. "But everybody knew you always came in second to Mrs. Smalley. You realized that if her pie went missing, you would be suspected."

"Right," Jazz said. "So you tried to distract everybody—by making them think the fair was jinxed. You figured if *lots* of things were going wrong, then nobody would pay much attention to one missing pie."

"That's why you pulled all those other pranks," Milo added. "The chickens. The switched CD. And—"

Jazz pulled the girl out from behind her. "The snake in the ball pit."

Winston took one look at the girl and crumbled.

"Okay," he confessed, "I did it. But

the pie contest wasn't fair! Everyone knew that—but no one would do anything about it! My pranks didn't hurt anyone. . . ."

"The chickens you let loose popped Uncle Sam," Jazz pointed out.

"I didn't mean for that to happen." Winston looked sad. "All I wanted was a fair shot at first prize. I know my chocolate-cookie cream pie is good!"

Milo thought longingly of his lost slice—that one crunchy, creamy, chocolatey bite. Winston *did* make good pie. *Really* good pie.

Reaching down under the table, Winston pulled out Mrs. Smalley's pie and put it back where it belonged.

Then he took his own pie off the table.

Gazing at it sadly, he said, "I guess I've disqualified myself. Sorry, chocolate pie. You should have been a winner."

He turned to leave.

Chief Smalley cleared his throat again.

"Not so fast, young man," he said.

"That's right, Jeffrey!" Mrs. Smalley cried. "ARREST HIM!"

The police chief looked at Winston sternly. "Later, you and I are going to have a long talk about these pranks."

Winston bit his lip and nodded.

"But right now," the chief went on, taking the pan from Winston's hands and setting it back on the table, "I'm here to *judge pie*."

Then he served himself a big slice, smiled, and dug in.

CHAPTER TEN

Milo lay back on the picnic blanket
and looked up at the darkening sky.
Nearby, Ethan and the snake girl played
dinosaurs, while the Zoo Crew—out of
costume now—tossed a Frisbee around
with Carlos and Spencer.

Next to Milo, Jazz read aloud her
letter to Dash Marlowe about how they
had solved The Case of the July 4th Jinx.

". . . and while Milo may not be so good at acting tough, everyone at the parade agreed that he made the pinkest, yummiest-looking strawberry they'd ever seen."

"*What?*" Milo sat up fast.

Jazz laughed. "Just making sure you were still listening. Don't worry, I left that last part out."

Winston appeared with his chocolate-cookie cream pie and a stack of paper plates. "Anybody want some pie?"

"ME!" they chorused.

Milo eagerly took a slice and

crammed it into his mouth. He wasn't taking any chances on losing more pie.

Jazz took a bite of her own slice, and then a bigger bite. "This is fantastic!" she said to Winston. "I can't *believe* your pie only got second place again."

Winston grinned. "Yeah, but it beats Mrs. Smalley's third."

"She looked pretty mad," Milo said.

"Oh, she cheered up when she found out the announcer job was open for next year. Now she is telling everyone she's meant for bigger things than pie."

Mrs. Smalley with a microphone? Milo thought. *Yikes!*

Just then, Chief Smalley strolled past, arm in arm with Viola Pritchett. Viola held a pie tin and a first place ribbon.

". . . best pie I ever tasted in my life,"
the chief was saying.

Viola Pritchett's large, pink face
turned even pinker. "Oh, Chief Smalley!"

The chief smiled. "Call me Jeff."

Jazz made a face, and Milo laughed.
Good thing Chief Smalley had decided
not to be the pie judge next year. It
would keep him out of trouble with his
new girlfriend.

Jazz swallowed her last bite of pie and
said to Winston, "I'm glad you're not mad
at us for busting you."

"Naw. I had it coming," Winston said.
"Besides, I've got to hand it to you—that
was pretty sharp detective work."

"We had it all wrong at first," Jazz said.
"If the Zoo Crew hadn't told us about

your pie getting second place three years in a row . . ."

"And if Jazz hadn't found the girl with the rubber snake—" Milo stopped and looked at her. "Where did you find her, anyway?"

Jazz smiled. "At the bake sale. I had it staked out. Remember yesterday, how she had all that chocolate on her face?"

Winston shook his head and joked, "Next time I bribe a little kid, I'll use something that's not so messy."

"What did Chief Smalley say to you?" Milo asked. "Are you in a lot of trouble?"

"I have to do twenty hours of community service," Winston said. Then he brightened. "But the chief told me I could volunteer at the after-school program. Teach the kids to bake."

Spotting Winston and his pie, the Frisbee players crowded onto the blanket along with Ethan and his new friend.

Carlos tagged after Crash, asking, "And did you really blow up the microwave in the teachers' lounge?"

"We didn't mean to," Crash said. "See, what happened was . . ."

Milo smiled to himself. Dash had been right that people weren't always what they seemed. The Zoo Crew hadn't turned out to be the rough, tough troublemakers he had imagined.

But that sure didn't make them safe to be around. If it wasn't a fire, it was a flood. If it wasn't a flood, it was an explosion—

BOOM! BOOM! BOOM!

Milo screamed, dove headfirst off the blanket, and rolled across the grass.

"Gosh, Milo," Ethan said, giggling and pointing at the sky. "It's only fireworks."

SUPER SLEUTHING STRATEGIES

A few days after Milo and Jazz wrote to Dash Marlowe, a letter arrived in the mail. . . .

Greetings, Milo and Jazz,

Great job! I'm glad the Zoo Crew turned out to be good guys. In my detecting career, when people are not what they seem, they usually turn out to be a lot *worse* than I expected. Someday I'll tell you about The Case of the Baby-Faced Burglar. . . .

Here are some other cases straight from my files. Some of them are not what they seem to be, either!

Happy Sleuthing!
—*Dash Marlowe*

Warm Up!
Get your brain good and limber with these Brain Stretchers! (The answers are at the end of the letter.)
1. Two men dove completely underwater. One man's hair got soaking wet. Why didn't the other man have wet hair too? (Note: Neither wore any kind of swim cap.)
2. What time of day is the same spelled forward and backward?
3. During a party, a girl says there is something in the room that everyone is able to touch with either their right or left hands, but you can only touch with your left hand. What is it?

90

The Take-Out Terror: A Mini-Mystery

Here's a mystery for you! Read the case, observe, and draw a conclusion. . . .

One dark and stormy Friday night, somebody tipped me off that the Take-Out Terror was going to rob a local restaurant. I had only one problem. My tipster didn't know which place would be hit: Pizza Patio, Sam's Steaks, or Meatball Maven.

The Terror always robbed restaurants the same way. He called in a phony take-out order, and when he arrived to pick up his food, he held the place up. Then he made off with the money—and a hot dinner.

But there were three restaurants to cover—and only one Dash Marlowe! All I had to go on were some menus. Luckily, that was enough. So—how did I know where the Take-Out Terror was going to strike?

Tempted: A Logic Puzzle

  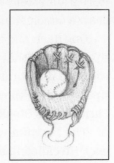

Three ex-robbers had given up their lives of crime, but sometimes they felt tempted to go back to their wicked ways. All three had special places to go and special things to do to help them stay honest. Can you figure out where each one went and what he did?

Read the clues and fill in the answer box where you can. Then read the clues again to fill in the rest.

	Rocky	Louie	Sal
Where he went			
What he did			

1. Rocky loved to sit by the lake.
2. One ex-robber had his own booth at Ice Cream Heaven and loved eating Double Fudge Delights.
3. Louie played catch with his mom.
4. The ex-robber who liked to cuddle with his dog, Fifi, was not Sal.
5. One ex-robber loved the park.

Answer: Rocky would sit by the lake and cuddle with his dog. Sal went to Ice Cream Heaven for a Double Fudge Delight. (Then he usually went to the gym.) Louie went to the park to play catch with his mom. She had a great curveball.

(Don't) Be Yourself: Role-Play

Going undercover isn't the only way a detective can use role-playing. Simply imagining what a suspect is thinking can help you crack a case. Picture yourself in these roles and sharpen your detecting skills! Use what you know about the person to predict what he or she would do.

1. You are Crash the day he went to the farm. Why did you pick up the baby goose?

    a. It was just adorable.

    b. I was hungry.

    c. I wanted to see webbed feet close up.

    d. It sounded fun at the time.

2. You are Carlos. Why did you spend so much time talking to Crash at the fireworks?

    a. I was after some trouble-making ideas.

    b. I wanted to seem tough.

    c. I was looking for a bodyguard.

    d. His stories were awesome.

3. You're in the Zoo Crew. Crash has a new idea that sounds pretty crazy. What do you do?

    a. Reason with him.

    b. Go along with it and hope we don't get in trouble.

    c. Distract him (with food).

    d. Tie him up.

(Milo, after you decide on your answers, how about checking with your friends to see if you were right? Let me know what you find out! –DM)

Now You See It . . . : An Observation Puzzle

Many's the time I solved a case by changing the way I looked at it. Take a look at these pictures. Then take another look. What do you see? (Remember: Things aren't always what they seem!)

1. Are the circles in the middle the same size?

2. What animal is this?

3. What word do you see?

4. Is one horizontal line longer?

Answers: 1. The circles in the middle are the same size. 2. It is a picture of a duck—and a rabbit! 3. The word CLUE is inside the word GOOD. 4. The horizontal lines are the same length.

Answers for Brain Stretchers: 1. He was bald. 2. Noon. 3. Your right elbow.

Dear Dash,

I showed everybody your role-playing questions and asked how they really felt.
1) Crash said definitely D. 2) Carlos said D.
3) I talked to a bunch of guys from the Zoo Crew, and they said the answer was B. Then they gave me a noogie.

Milo

"**The Milo & Jazz Mysteries** are highly recommended additions to school and community library collections for young readers."
—*Midwest Book Review*

Titles in *The Milo & Jazz Mysteries* series:

The Case of the Stinky Socks

The Case of the Poisoned Pig

The Case of the *Haunted* Haunted House

The Case of the Amazing Zelda

The Case of the July 4th Jinx

The Case of the Missing Moose

The Case of the Purple Pool

The Case of the Diamonds in the Desk

The Case of the Crooked Campaign

COMING January 2013
The Case of the Superstar Scam

Visit www.kanepress.com
to see all titles in
The Milo & Jazz Mysteries.

ABOUT THE AUTHOR

Lewis B. Montgomery is the pen name of a writer whose favorite authors include CSL, EBW, and LMM. Those initials are a clue—but there's another clue, too. Can you figure out their names?

Besides writing the Milo & Jazz mysteries, LBM enjoys eating spicy Thai noodles and blueberry ice cream, riding a bike, and reading. Not all at the same time, of course. At least, not anymore. But that's another story. . . .

ABOUT THE ILLUSTRATOR

Amy Wummer has illustrated more than 50 children's books. She uses pencils, watercolors, and ink—but not the invisible kind.

Amy and her husband, who is also an artist, live in Pennsylvania . . . in a mysterious old house which has a secret hidden room in the basement!